Dearest Lily!,
Happy Birthday!
May you lead your life with
your generous, beautiful heart.
Love,
Jennifer

ISBN: 1-4392-1654-1

ISBN-13: 9781439216545

Visit www.booksurge.com to order additional copies.

A Queendom Blessed by Grace

Creating a Beautiful World with a Kind and Generous Heart!

Written by Jennifer R. Lazinsk
Illustrated by Giovanna Adams

This book is dedicated to my beautiful husband, Harvey, who is my inspiration, fellow journeyman, consumate cheerleader and true north, and our delicious daughter, Jordana, who is my muse and grace, and who embodies joy, kindness, divine spirit and radiant light.

JRL

To Wes, Grace, Logan and the "muse" for the inspiration that they give to me each day.

GA

The amazing beauty of the Queendom of Plentitude stretched as far as the eye could see. Fragrant and huge flowers burst open at the first sign of Spring, and dazzling, rainbow colored butterflies joyfully soared through the sky.

The gigantic fruits and vegetables grew so deliciously sweet and juicy that they turned children's cheeks a glorious shade of pink. Every person who had ever visited Plentitude was in awe of its splendor.

Princess Grace, Plentitude's kind and joyful princess, was adored by all because of her loving heart. Her sparkling brown eyes held a deep respect for every living creature, and her beautiful, radiant smile shined generously for the whole world to see.

Grace was different from other princesses in so many ways. Firstly, she always carried a sparkling, purple staff with a shiny red heart at its tip that her grandma had given Grace when she was four years old. *"We all hold a brilliant light deep within our hearts,"* Grace's grandma said when she gave her the staff. *"Take this staff as a reminder to fill the world with love and joy, and let the kindness in your heart shine for everyone to see."* Grace's grandma also taught her a little rhyme that she sang when she had carried the staff, **"I am here, so there's nothing to fear, how can I help you my dear?"** Grace loved the staff and the rhyme so much, and promised that she would always carry the staff in her hands and the rhyme in her heart.

Grace also looked like no other princess. Her wild, curly, brown hair had a personality all its own. And no matter how hard she tried, Princess Grace just couldn't keep her princess clothes clean. With reckless abandon, Grace would run as fast as she could to help anyone in need, splashing through the thick mud and shimmering streams, her sparkling staff leading the way, singing at the top of her lungs, ***"I am here, so there's nothing to fear, how can I help you my dear?"*** As busy a princess as she was, whenever anyone was hurt or in trouble, she would tend to their scrapes and bruises, listen to what frightened them, and give them comfort for as long as they needed. More often than not, though, the mere sight of their breathless, curly-headed, muddy princess would make people burst out laughing and forget about their troubles.

So, you see, no one who lived in Plentitude was surprised by the queendom's beauty, because everyone knew that Princess Grace's generous heart and loving ways caused spectacular things to happen around her.

Nearby there was a very different kind of Queendom called Nojoya, in which lived Princess Grace's godsister, the unkind and jealous Princess Gwendyl. Gwendyl's negative spirit cast a dark shadow over her queendom. *"Leave me alone, take care of your own problems; I don't have time for you!"* Gwendyl would often say. Gwendyl only had time for herself, and looking after her crisply pressed clothing, perfectly polished nails, and the many glittering jewels she loved to buy for herself.

Flowers and trees wouldn't grow in Nojoya. The once deep, flowing streams and rivers had all dried up, the bunnies, chipmunks, and squirrels had all run away, and the happy sounds of children playing hopscotch, skipping rope, and singing songs were nowhere to be heard. The brown and barren Nojoya reflected Gwendyl's unhappy heart.

Grace and Gwendyl had loved one another so much when they were very small girls. They would play princess dress-up together for hours each day under the enchanted deep purple sky, and they would play until the glistening sun had long set.

Together, Grace and Gwendyl held hands, danced, and sang; all the while dreaming of the day that they would be the princesses of two glorious queendoms, living side-by-side. But as time passed by the differences between Grace and Gwendyl began to slowly separate their hearts.

Starting from the time she was a little girl, Grace would joyfully skip through the woods while watering and gently stroking the soft, blossoming lilacs and lavender, exclaiming *"Oh, you are so beautiful; you make my life rich with your yummy smells!"* When she sensed a dog, bird, deer, or horse that needed help, Grace would sprint towards her as fast as she could, singing ***"I am here, so there's nothing to***

fear, how can I help you my dear?" She'd then scoop her up and love her back to health with food and tender kisses and hugs. Grace appreciated her life and was grateful for what she had, and she spread her love and joy wherever she could. Throughout her life, every living thing wanted to give back to her for all of the kindness she had always given to them.

From the time *Gwendyl* was a little girl, she lived each day thinking *only* of her own needs.

Gwendyl would walk right by a crying child or a bird with a broken wing, and pretend not to hear a person calling for help. *"Not today, gotta be on my way!"* Gwendyl would shout as she busily scurried along. Gwendyl's grandma had *also* given her a purple, sparkly staff with a red heart at its tip, and taught her the special rhyme. Even though Gwendyl loved her grandma, she decided that the rhyme was silly and she never gave it a second thought. And the special staff soon became buried and forgotten among Gwendyl's piles of unused toys.

Sadly, when Gwendyl grew up and became princess, she was overcome with anger and jealousy at Plentitude's rich beauty. *"Grace must have put her whole queendom under a magic spell in order for it to be so wonderful!"* Gwendyl thought to herself.

Determined to have Nojoya be as beautiful as Plentitude, one night Princess Gwendyl thought to herself, *"I'm going into Plentitude's gardens and I'm going to take the flower seeds and colorful butterflies that Grace has cast a spell upon so that I can have a gorgeous queendom too!"* Gwendyl dressed in a black cloak in order to blend in with the night sky, she then climbed over Plentitude's front gate.

Spotting a beautiful field of sunflowers, Gwendyl quickly scooped up as many seeds as she could and stuffed them in her pockets. She then dashed to Plentitude's magnificent butterfly garden where she caught the biggest, brightest, orange butterflies she had ever seen. After returning to Nojoya, she planted the seeds and set the butterflies free in her queendom's empty gardens.

Gwendyl waited impatiently for the seeds to grow and for the butterflies to flourish. But the weeks passed by and there were no signs of life from the tiny seeds, and the once gorgeous butterflies began to whither and turn gray.

Gwendyl became confused, yet she was still more determined then ever to capture Plentitude's beauty.

*"Since the magic of Plentitude's magnificence obviously doesn't lie in the seeds or butterflies, the secret **must** lie within Grace's purple staff" Gwendyl exclaimed. "If I can just steal her staff, I **know** that I can easily change the fate of my queendom and **I** will have the most magnificent queendom of all! But everyone knows that Grace never let's the staff leave her side, so I must capture Grace too!"*

So Princess Gwendyl, this time dressed in her own pressed clothes, calmly walked into Plentitude demanding to speak to her godsister. When Grace walked towards her, Gwendyl shouted, *"I know what you are doing Grace. I know that you are casting spells over everything in your queendom, and now it's my turn to use the magic staff!"* Before anyone knew what was happening, Gwendyl had managed to grab Grace **and** her purple sparkling staff. In a flurry of dust and confusion, the people of Plentitude were left with only the echoing sounds of Plentitude's gates closing with a loud **CRASH!!!** Their beloved Princess Grace was gone!!!!!

Grace was stunned that her godsister was doing this, and she tried desperately to convince Gwendyl that neither she nor her purple staff held any magical powers at all. She begged over and over, *"Please Gwendyl, let me go back to Plentitude; it's my home!"* She reminded Gwendyl of the time when their grandma had given both of them a staff as a gift. *"Remember Gwendyl,"* Grace exclaimed, *"Remember when grandma gave us the staffs as a reminder to fill the world with love and joy?"*

"*Grace, those days are long past now*" Gwendyl exclaimed.
"*Yes, I remember that the staff was from grandma, but I also
believe that **it** must be what holds the magical powers!*"
Gwendyl then ordered her guards to throw Grace into a
small, cold cell. "*I will learn everything I can from you and the
magic staff and then send you away forever!*" Grace became
extremely afraid.

But as the days and weeks passed, Grace still maintained
her beautiful, gentle, and kind spirit despite being confined
to the small cell. Gwendyl kept trying to weaken Grace into
revealing the "secret and magical powers" of the purple staff,
but, instead, Grace kept softly repeating that the staff was
not magic and reminding Gwendyl of how they had once
loved one another. Gwendyl's heart started to soften, but,
nevertheless, she continued her failed attempts to awaken
the "magic" in Grace's staff, that *still* lay lifeless in Gwendyl's
hands.

Then one quiet afternoon, while passing the cell, Gwendyl heard Grace's soft voice coming from inside. *"Who can she be talking to?* Gwendyl wondered aloud. She then hid outside the wall and was able to hear Grace softly singing, **"I am here, so there's nothing to fear, how can I help you my dear?"** she continued, *"Come here precious, hungry, little mouse, come here and take this food"* she heard Grace whisper.

And then, peeking into the small window of her cell, Gwendyl saw Grace pick up the tiny mouse and begin to stroke and kiss her head. Gwendyl, in disbelief, cried aloud, *"How can this be? Could she really be so generous that she would give a **lowly** mouse her last, small ration of food? That she would kiss, stroke and even sing to a **mere** mouse?"* Gwendyl was left speechless.

It was at that moment that Gwendyl remembered the sound of her grandma's sweet voice singing to *her* that same rhyme Grace had been singing to the *mouse*. She then allowed herself to also remember how Grace, from the time *she* was a child, had lived her life generously and always seemed to be *looking* for ways to help all living creatures.

Suddenly, Gwendyl's hardened, jealous heart burst open, and she finally understood that there was never any magic in the staff after all, but it was purely Grace's kind and loving heart that created the bounty found in the glorious world that surrounded her.

With a changed heart, Gwendyl jumped out from behind the wall and exclaimed, *"I feel ashamed of how I treated you Grace! I only wanted Nojoya to be as beautiful as Plentitude, but now I finally understand why your queendom outshines all the others!"* She flung open the locked door, and Grace quietly wrapped Gwendyl in a warm embrace.

And so it went, that even though she was free to return to her beloved queendom, Grace remained in Nojoya for several more weeks because she knew she was needed there.

She spent time walking the grounds, watering the tiny seedlings, looking for ways to help, and running through the streams with messy clothes, mud-caked curls, and her sparkling staff held firmly in her hand, singing, ***"I am here, so there's nothing to fear, how can I help you my dear?"*** to anyone in need.

And slowly but surely, in the once gray, cold and joyless Queendom of Nojoya, the flowers began to explode in all of the magnificent colors of the rainbow. One by one the animals happily returned, and, once again, children's laughter began to fill the land. With Princess Gwendyl having watched and learned, it was finally time for Grace to return home.

As Grace was preparing to leave, she turned to Gwendyl and handed the sparkling purple staff to her, *"You take it now, it's your turn godsister"* Grace said, *"Grandma would have wanted it this way."*

When Grace turned to look back at Nojoya for the last time, she could hear faint echoes of *"I am here, so there's nothing to fear, how can I help you my dear?"* being lovingly sung from person to person off in the distance.

With a simple nod and gentle smile from Grace, Princess
Gwendyl and all of the people and animals of Nojoya gathered
around to embrace Grace and to accompany her home.

When they arrived, the people of Plentitude welcomed their loving Princess, her new friends, and her godsister with a celebration that would be remembered until the end of time.

The two queendoms, Plentitude and Joya, living as
neighbors, spent the rest of their days in perfect, bountiful
and glorious harmony.

Made in the USA
Middletown, DE
21 September 2023

38899602R00020